He wasn't worth a minute of her time, especially after what he'd done to her...so why was she crying?

Ignoring her growling stomach, Lexi found a pair of stretchy shorts and a Mackinac Island T-shirt and pulled them on, sans bra. Luke had stashed her overnight bag and purse someplace in his truck. Donning a pair of flip-flops, she looked outside the bedroom window. The rain had slowed to a light drizzle.

Hoping Luke had left his truck unlocked so she could get her suitcase, she opened the window, jimmied open the screen, and crawled out. Sloshing through the mud, she ignored the sharp ache of leaving Luke.

She tried the driver's door of the truck. It was unlocked. Reaching into the backseat she found her case and purse underneath her wedding dress. She shut the door as softly as she could, cursing herself for caring if Luke's leather upholstery got wet, then set off toward the road. Her tears started, soon followed by wrenching sobs. Not for Marcus, but at the thought of never seeing Luke again.

What was wrong with her? Luke was deranged and unhinged. Why did she still love him? She needed psychological help. She stopped to get a better grip on her suitcase and screamed as two hands grabbed her from behind, taking a firm hold on her waist.

She's filled with a sense of dread on her wedding day…

Lexi McCardle still dreams of Luke Kettering, the guy who dumped her in high school, although she hasn't seen or heard from him since. Concerned about her wedding-day jitters, her family questions her decision to go through with it. Then her fiancé calls it off just as she's kidnapped by Luke. Luke says he loves her and always has. But she doesn't believe him. Can she ever get past her feelings of hurt and betrayal in order to trust him again?

He's tried to forget her, but to no avail…

After he learns of Lexi's wedding plans on social media, Luke calls in all his favors through his contacts with the prosecutor's office where he works and discovers a dark secret about her fiancé, forcing the man to call off the wedding. Luke then kidnaps Lexi and takes her to a remote cabin in Northern Michigan to give them some time alone. He's always loved her, but even as the passion ignites between them, he fears they can never get past her anger. Can he convince her that she belongs to him, or will his betrayal in high school doom their love forever?

KUDOS for *Reclaiming Lexi*

In *Reclaiming Lexi* by Tara Eldana, Lexi gets dump by her fiancé on her wedding day and is kidnapped by her old boyfriend Luke, whom she hasn't seen since high school. Not only does Luke kidnap her and take her to a cabin in the mountains, he confesses that he made her fiancé call off the wedding. Needless to say, Lexi is pissed. However, she has never gotten over Luke and wasn't sure that she should go through with the wedding anyway, so she doesn't resist all that hard. As this is a steamy romance, it's my kind of book. The sex scenes are hot, and the action is fast-paced. The only thing wrong with the story is that it ends much too soon. ~ *Taylor Jones, Reviewer*

Reclaiming Lexi by Tara Eldana is a cute, clever, and hot steamy romance. Our heroine, Lexi McCurdle is getting married, or at least she thought she was. Although she is dreading it, she assumes that her fears are just normal jitters. Then her finance sends her a text, telling her there is someone else. On her wedding day! He couldn't have told her this sooner? Or in person? Then, as she is left reeling from the shock of having her wedding called off when she is just about to leave for the church, she gets kidnapped by Luke Kettering, her old flame from high school. Lexi hasn't seen Luke for eight years but she has never forgotten him, or forgiven him for dumping her after only dating her for three weeks. Now Luke is suddenly back in her life, and he seems determined to stay there. *Reclaiming Lexi* is short, even for a novella, but Eldana packs a lot into the story. The characters are charming and intriguing, the plot strong, the sex scenes hot and steamy. What's not to love? *~ Regan Murphy, Reviewer*

ACKNOWLEDGEMENTS

To my mother, for reading to me, to my father, for his wonderful stories and to my husband Tom and children Tina and Tommy, for supporting their absentee wife and mother who had her nose stuck in a book or at a computer screen.

To Lauri Wellington at Black Opal Books, for giving me a chance to tell my stories, editors Shannon Zweig and fabulous Faith for shaping it up and Jack for his amazing cover.

To my beta readers Deb King, Susana Woloson, and Maria Allard for giving me the confidence to keep trying.

And to the Greater Detroit Romance Writers of America, I would never be a published author if not for your invaluable support and guidance. You ladies rock.

Reclaiming Lexi

Tara Eldana

A Black Opal Books Publication

GENRE: STEAMY ROMANCE/WOMEN'S FICTION/CONTEMPO-RARY ROMANCE

RECLAIMING LEXI
Copyright © 2015 by Tara Eldana
Cover Design by Jackson Cover Design
All cover art copyright © 2015
All Rights Reserved
Print ISBN: 978-1-626943-62-9

First Publication: OCTOBER 2015

Published by Black Opal Books **http://www.blackopalbooks.com**

DEDICATION

To all those who believe
there really is a happily ever after.

Chapter 1

"Are you sure?" her mother asked.

Lexi McCardle fidgeted with the beading on her ivory gown, fighting to breathe through the tightness in her chest. She met her parents' worried gazes then glanced at the clock in the kitchen of the home she grew up in. In true Michigan fashion, calm skies that had blazed sunny blue two hours ago were now gusting an ugly shade of greenish gray.

The impending storm matched the turmoil brewing inside of her. She was getting married in one hour. She would stand in the church where she and her sisters were baptized. She would pledge her body and heart to Marcus in front of 150 of their family and friends. Unfortunately, she couldn't get her mind off Luke, the senior she dated in high school for all of three weeks, until he dumped her ass and fucked his way through the rest of her sophomore class, with the exception of her.

She hadn't seen him since high school. Eight years later and he still haunted her dreams, like the one last night. It should be Marcus, not Luke Kettering making her heart pound. Marcus made her feel calm and safe. Thoughts of Luke made her restless and edgy. She was pathetic.

Lexi and Marcus had dated for two years before he proposed on their college graduation day, promising he would upgrade her diamond as soon as he was working. As always, he'd kept his promise. So what if his kisses didn't make her blood sing? He always kept his promises, but now Lexi wanted to break her promise to marry him.

"Don't do it," hissed her younger sister Kenzie, a senior in high school. "And not just so I don't have to wear this God-awful dress."

"Kenzie." Mary McCardle softly chided her youngest daughter, but her tone meant major business.

Reeni, her middle sister, squeezed Lexi's hand.

"These are just jitters, right? This feeling of sick dread in the pit of my stomach is normal, isn't it?" Lexi didn't realize she spoke out loud until her mother grabbed her other hand.

"No, sweets, it isn't," her mother said.

Lexi's cell phone pinged. It was a text from Marcus. *Sorry, Lex.*

She stared at the words, and texted back. *Sorry 4 what?*

I can't. There's someone else.

Lexi set her phone on the kitchen table next to her bridal bouquet of white roses. The perfect, expensive blooms seemed obscene.

"Lexi?" Reeni picked up the phone and then let loose with string of expletives Lexi didn't have the nerve to say in front of their father.

"What?" John McCardle demanded.

Kenzie took the phone from Reeni and, together, she and their father read it. John yanked off his bow tie and then slammed his fist on the kitchen counter. Reeni held the phone out for Mary to read.

"Douche bag couldn't tell you to your face," Kenzie growled.

Lexi thought of everyone waiting at the church and the food her parents had paid for and turned panicked eyes on her mother. "Mom?"

"We'll deal." Mary took off her pink orchid corsage and threw it across the kitchen. "You stay here."

⋐⋑⋐⋑

Luke watched Lexi's family storm out to the Buick

in their driveway and speed off. He'd been watching the house like some crazed stalker since dawn. Since no one else had left, Lexi should still be inside. Unless she'd spent the night someplace else.

Taking a chance she was still there, he walked up to the front door, turned the knob as if he had every right, and walked into her house.

Lexi stood in front of the fireplace, staring at her cell phone, unaware of his presence.

Her breasts and hips had filled out in the last eight years. Her cheeks had lost a bit of the round fullness, but it only made her more beautiful. Her blonde hair hung in waves, and her turquoise eyes reminded him of the waters in the Caribbean. The same stunning eyes and face he saw every time he fucked a woman.

She looked like an angel in her dress. And he wanted to rip it to shreds because she bought it to marry someone else.

Chapter 2

L exi caught sight of Luke then clutched her chest and shrieked.

She had to be dreaming again, but her shoes pinched her toes and the weight of her wedding gown pressed against her ribs. His chocolate brown eyes flashed with anger, and the stubble on his jaw glinted in the afternoon sun. How was that possible? She never dreamt in color.

Even his scent wafted across the room like a lake breeze mixed with pine needles.

"Waiting for your ride?" He didn't wait for her answer, but stalked toward her, hoisted her over his shoulder, and headed back to her front door. "The wedding's off," he said flatly.

"How'd you—" She clamped her mouth shut. She was humiliated enough.

"Yours?" He reached down, without dropping her, to pick up a small suitcase. Without waiting for her answer, he walked out the front door. The street was empty, because all her neighbors were waiting at the church. He tossed her into a white Yukon with tinted windows, locked her in, and then tossed her suitcase into the back seat. Before she could escape, he got into the driver's seat. He snatched her cell phone out of her hand and threw it out the window.

"Hey!" she shrieked.

"You won't need it," he said.

"My family—"

"We can call them later."

"We? There is no we," she screamed, so loud her throat hurt. "We haven't spoken in eight years! Why now? What are you doing?"

He stopped at a red light, and growled, "Take that damned dress off." He reached in the back seat and then tossed a Red Wings jersey onto her lap.

When the light turned green, he floored it. "Buckle up."

Gunning the accelerator, he merged onto I-75, heading north, and stared straight ahead. He ignored her until they pulled into an abandoned truck weight station. This was her chance to get away from this insanity. Her heart pounding as the SUV rocked to a stop, she scrambled for the door lock. Before she could escape, he unbuckled her seat belt, grabbed her shoulders, and pulled her toward him so her ass was on the console. Trapped with her back to him, she could do nothing as he undid the first few buttons on the top of her sleeveless bridal gown. He gave a frustrated growl then pulled hard, ripping the rest of the dress off.

"You're insane," she gasped.

He pulled her into his lap and yanked her dress over her legs, tearing it off before tossing it onto the backseat. He then pulled her ballet-style shoes off, shoved them in the glove box, and then locked it.

Panicked, she could only pant. Was he some crazed murderer? Christ, she could feel his erection. "What the hell are you doing?"

"Stopping something I should have way before now." He lightly grazed the skin above her elbow and she went boneless. Her sex clenched in long-denied need, drenching her lacy blue thong. There was no way he could miss her arousal. He pressed his mouth to her neck and sucked hard, marking her. He pushed her strapless bra down to her waist.

Why was she letting him do this? She was pathetic. She fought back a sob. Her nipples pebbled, and he pinched them. She stifled a moan at the familiar touch.

For the love of God, what was wrong with her? She

was still a virgin because, after Luke, the thought of someone else, even Marcus, made her stomach clench. And Luke hadn't spared her a breath since high school.

"I'm not doing this." She jerked away from him and pulled the jersey on.

"Didn't spare you a breath?" Luke asked.

Had she said that out loud? She *had* to stop doing that.

He gripped the steering wheel and stared straight ahead. "You don't have a fucking clue." He pulled out of the truck stop and got back on northbound I-75.

She shook with nerves and wanting him. "No fucking clue? Spare me. You fucked so many girls I lost count."

But she hadn't. Every girl linked to him added a layer to the ice Lexi encased herself in. She'd heard "cold bitch" and "cock tease" from most of the guys she'd tried to be with. Until Marcus. Patient and gentle Marcus, who promised to wait until she was ready to belong to him. And even he had eventually dumped her for someone else.

She couldn't blame him.

A call came through on Luke's cell phone syncing through his stereo. "Text me, okay?" he said.

Luke looked at Lexi then pushed the button to disconnect the call. Lexi read the text before Luke snatched his phone. It said "He sent the text."

"My parents—" Lexi began. "I have to let them know. Just take me back."

"Forget it." But he handed her his cell phone. "Call them."

"So you can hear every word?'

"Yup."

"Fuck."

She dialed Reeni. It went to voice mail. "I'm okay," Lexi glared at Luke. "I'm with Luke Kettering, f—from high school." Tears coursed down her cheeks.

Luke disconnected the call from his steering wheel. She turned away from him and took deep breaths. Only when she thought she could trust her voice, did she set his phone in the center console and turn to face him.

"What are you playing at?" she asked softly. "Courtroom drama isn't enough for you?" She'd heard he landed a position in the prosecutor's office right out of law school. Big surprise. Everything came easy for him.

"I'm not playing." His laugh was bitter. "As for drama, I'm the lowest position on the food chain. All I get right now is drunk driving cases." He took his gaze off the road for a second, anger adding gold lights to his brown eyes. He picked up his phone, turned it off, and slid it into his pocket. "There's water in the back seat, if you want it."

She unbuckled her seatbelt, scooched up on her

knees, and reached back. The jersey rode up, no doubt giving him a clear view of her lacy blue thong.

He sucked in a sharp breath before he braked and swerved, slamming her against the door. "Fuck." He grabbed her arm and hauled her onto her seat. "You okay?" He didn't take his gaze off the freeway.

"Define okay," she said. Her hip hurt.

"Fuck." He pulled off the freeway into an empty commuter carpool parking lot, opened his door, and sprinted around to her door. He yanked it open and lifted her into his arms, hooking her legs around his waist like he owned her. She let him.

He strode across the lot, lowered her onto a wooden bench, and lifted her jersey, running his hand over her achy hip.

She shivered and tried to pull away from him. "I'm okay," she said.

Ignoring her, he stepped away, pulled out his phone, and dialed.

Barefoot, she was effectively trapped on the bench.

"Mr. McCardle, this is Luke Kettering. Lexi's with me...Yes, the asshole from high school...I'm in the prosecutor's office, my job is, I mean...Oakland County. I'm an attorney."

Luke paced a few steps away and she couldn't hear what he said. It wasn't long before he gave her the phone.

Her mother and sisters all screamed through the speakerphone at once.

"Alexis Marie, are you okay?" Her mother's voice rose above her sisters'.

Just peachy, considering she was barefoot in an empty parking lot with a guy she'd never gotten over, and who was playing some sort of sick game with her.

"I'm okay, Mumma, I promise." Her voice sounded stronger than she felt.

Eavesdropping shamelessly, Luke's eyes blazed with approval, which pleased her ridiculously.

"I'm sorry I left you to deal with the mess," she said.

"The douchebag made the announcement," Kenzie said.

"Language, Kenzie," her mother said. The call dropped then. Lexi called back, but the voices were sketchy. "Love you," she said loudly just before it cut out again.

Luke stalked back to her and pointed to a port-a-john. "Do you?"

She shook her head. "Not that bad."

He chuckled. It was the first time they'd smiled at each other since he strode into her parents' house.

He lifted her and she wrapped her legs around his waist.

Why couldn't she resist him? Where was he taking

her? She had to get away from him so she could think straight. Why did he affect her so strongly?

Chapter 3

Luke set her on the passenger seat and inspected her feet before he massaged first one, then the other.

Lexi bit back something between a sigh and a moan. Damn, he was good at that. The enticing scent of his aftershave wafted to her nostrils, causing her sex to react, soaking her thong, again. She squirmed on the seat. Luke lifted the side of the jersey revealing the scrap of blue lace.

Thunder rumbled in the distance.

"The rain is following us," Lexi said, nervously. "Smell it, the ozone, I mean."

"Christ, Lexi." He claimed her mouth in a hard, angry kiss. "All I can smell is you."

಄಄಄

Luke hooked his finger through the strap of her thong and yanked until the lace ripped—lust, and something else, burning through him. "You wore them for him."

He pulled the scraps of silk free while outside lightning cracked. She tugged the jersey over her butt as he buckled her seatbelt. Sitting back, he held the thong to his face, watching her. Lightning crackled and he shut her door, breaking the intense staring contest.

He got back in the driver's seat and peeled out of the truck stop, just as torrential rain painted fat drops on the windshield.

"You're insane," she muttered.

Was he? They'd warned him in the prosecutor's office that some people couldn't take seeing the underbelly of human nature day after day. Luke had prosecuted more drunk driving cases than he could count over the last few months. Many of them had been second- and third-time offenders, and one man had his young child with him in the car when he police had pulled him over at three in the morning. He caught one really bad case, meth-head parents who neglected their child. The toddler had died with sores all over his body. And when he'd seen Lexi's friend Emma's post online about Lexi's wedding, he'd snapped.

He called in every favor and wielded his meager in-fluence as a low-ranking assistant prosecutor to dig up the shit on the *asshat* Lexi was to marry. Then he co-erced the dick to call off the wedding. It had been pure dumb luck that he found her alone in her parent's house today.

"This is fucked," Lexi said, glaring at him.

"Language, Lex," he said, mimicking her mother.

She set her mouth in a hard line, which made him want to haul her into his arms and kiss her.

"Lex? You don't get to call me that. Nor do you get to lecture me on my filthy mouth, Lucas," she hissed the name she knew he hated. "For the love of God, where are we going? And give me my shoes, dammit."

He wanted her barefoot, barefoot and pregnant, he realized. The startling thought hit him like a punch to the gut. "When we get there," he said.

The thought of her belly round with his baby made him hard and he squirmed in his seat.

"Get where?" She stretched her legs out, circling first one ankle, then the other. The innately feminine action made him even harder. He stared straight ahead. The rain was letting up.

After a few miles she shut her eyes then fell asleep, her hands still clutching the hem of the jersey. She was still sound asleep when he pulled up to his uncle's cabin at the edge of the national forest. His uncle had been there a couple of weeks ago, so the freezer and cupboards would be well stocked.

He quietly opened the front door of the cabin and left it slightly ajar. Then he went back, gathered Lexi in his arms, and carried her inside. She roused as he slammed the door shut. "We're home, babe."

"Luke?" she said in a drowsy voice. "I thought I dreamed you again."

Again? "Again, babe?"

"N—no, I mean, I'm not your b—babe," she sputtered.

He held her against him as she slid her feet to the ground. "Yes, Lexi, you are," he said, his mouth inches from hers. "Mine, that is. I knew it in high school but I fucked up, a mistake I won't make again."

"You fucked your way—" Lexi began, her eyes blazing gray before he took hold of her chin, cutting her off.

"I only saw your face. And more than once called out your name."

Chapter 4

Lexi gasped. Luke fused his mouth to hers. Her hands slipped under his shirt, caressing his rock hard abs. He'd filled out since high school. His shoulders and chest were broader now and there was a smattering of hair on his chest that arrowed lower than she remembered.

He broke off the kiss and took hold of her left hand. "Take it off." He glared at her engagement ring and tweaked her nipple with his free hand.

Wondering why she was doing what he wanted, she slipped if off. He took it from her nerveless fingers, walked to the front door, and threw into a stand of trees.

"Luke?" She ran to the front door. "I need to return that. He spent—"

"No," he said quietly. "I'll write him a check. Anything else he gave you, get rid of it. You belong to me."

"You're delusional," she said as he advanced toward her. "Bathroom?" she squeaked. "I need to."

He pointed down a short hallway and she scrambled to the tiny room, trying to lock the door, but there was no lock.

"You can't hide from me, Lexi," he said from the other side of the door.

Holy hell. She sat on the spotless toilet for a long time, regretting the Brazilian wax Kenzie dared her to get. She felt too vulnerable and exposed to Luke as it was.

The knob rattled and turned. "Time's up, babe."

"I'm not—" The words died in her throat when he flung the door open. She was still sitting on the toilet, the jersey bunched at her waist, giving him a glimpse of her bare mound. He stared at her bare flesh and she heard his sharp intake of breath. She pulled the jersey down then tried to brush past him to wash her hands.

"Christ, Lexi." He caught hold of her waist and pushed her against the wall. His hand delving under the jersey and to her smooth mound.

"Has he seen this?" His eyes blazed into hers as he slipped a finger inside her.

How could she be wet? She shook her head and shut her eyes.

Why was she answering him? And why was she rubbing against him?

"God you are so wet and so tight." He moved his thumb to her swollen nub and she bucked. She needed his touch more than she needed her next breath.

"Look at me, Lexi."

His gruff command had her watching his face as he stroked his thumb harder and harder until the starburst exploded and she screamed his name. Her knees turned to water, but Luke kept a firm hold on her, pressing her face into the cords of his neck.

She inhaled his scent, which calmed and excited her in equal parts.

Why did this feel so right, like she belonged in his arms? He hadn't acknowledged her existence for eight years. She was like a pathetic puppy lapping up the scraps of attention he was meting out.

She reached for the icy mantle of dead calm she'd perfected since he dumped her in high school, gathering it close, and straightened her spine.

"I need my shoes," she said. "And something else to wear home, which is where I'm going—now."

꒰꒱꒰

Lexi shut down on him. Luke was both pissed and proud of her strength. He loved that fire in her eyes.

Loved how her luscious body had blossomed into soft feminine curves. Loved the blogs, short stories, and poems she'd published online. She'd become a brilliant writer.

"We're not leaving. Clothes are in the closet. Shoes too. I'll make lunch." He glanced at his cell phone. "Or dinner."

"You cook?" she asked.

He shrugged. "It relaxes me."

She crossed her arms in front of her chest. "I need to leave."

He strode over to her, picked her up, and set her delectable ass on the kitchen counter. He moved between her legs and covered her slit, damp with her juices, with his palm. "No. You. Don't." Craving her taste, he fused his mouth to hers. He lifted his head, freeing her lips, and slipped his fingers, wet with her juices, into her open mouth. "Suck," he demanded. "Taste how you want me."

She did. His cock hardened, straining against his fly. Her blue eyes took on a deeper midnight blue cast. He remembered that color, it used to mean she wanted him. If he was lucky, it still did. Still, he wanted all of her. Could she forgive him for letting her go and staying away from her for so long? Could he forgive himself and be what she needed?

Rain pounded the cabin and thunder rumbled. His

questions were dark as the skies. He pulled back, leaving her on the counter. Hunger gnawed at him. She had to be famished, too. He took some eggs and bacon out of the fridge and washed his hands.

Lexi chewed on a knuckle, revealing her worry. The bacon hissed in the pan. He pulled out a loaf of sliced French bread from the freezer and threw it like a football to her. She caught it easily.

"Toast." He pointed to the old toaster oven. "No butter, but there's homemade strawberry jam."

She stared at him like he lost his mind.

"Down." He lifted her off the counter and set her bare feet on the linoleum. He wanted to spread that jam on her jutting nipples and lick it off. Instead, he swatted her bottom.

"Oww." She scurried away, but not before her eyes went dark blue. Even pissed as hell, she was fucking perfect for him.

And she thought Matt or Mike or Marc…whatever his name was…had dumped her. Did she know her ex-fiancé swung both ways? Did she suspect Luke had forced him to call the wedding off? She'd glanced at the text before he could grab his phone.

e/se/s

Lexi gently pried the frozen slices of bread apart,

put them on the rack in oven, and set it to toast, as Luke had ordered.

Obviously he hadn't lost his take-charge attitude, the same attitude that had led him to be captain of the track team and vice president of the student congress in high school. She usually chafed at being bossed around. Hell, she was the bossy older sister.

Marcus had been happy to let her take charge of their wedding plans, their social life, even what they did or didn't do sexually. If she was honest, mostly what they didn't do. She never simmered for Marcus's touch as she had and did for Luke's. Marcus never took quick, decisive action. She worried her lower lip. Like calling off the wedding. Granted she was relieved he had, but she was damned if she'd clue Luke into that fact. Besides, she was through taking orders from him. The oven pinged.

"All done." She stomped out of the kitchen in search of clothes and her overnight bag. She had to get back to the shambles of her life.

Ignoring her growling stomach, she found a pair of stretchy shorts and a Mackinac Island T-shirt and pulled them on, sans bra. Luke had stashed her overnight bag and purse someplace in his truck. Donning a pair of flip-flops, she looked outside the bedroom window. The rain had slowed to a light drizzle.

Hoping Luke had left his truck unlocked so she

could get her suitcase, she opened the window, jimmied open the screen, and crawled out. Sloshing through the mud, she ignored the sharp ache of leaving Luke.

She tried the driver's door of the truck. It was unlocked. Reaching into the backseat she found her case underneath her wedding dress. She shut the door as softly as she could, cursing herself for caring if Luke's leather upholstery got wet, then set off toward the road. Her tears started, soon followed by wrenching sobs. Not for Marcus, but at the thought of never seeing Luke again.

What was wrong with her? Luke was deranged and unhinged. Why did she still love him? She needed psychological help. She stopped to get a better grip on her suitcase and screamed as two hands grabbed her from behind, taking a firm hold on her waist.

Chapter 5

Recognizing Luke's touch as he pulled her into his chest, Lexi let go of the suitcase and sagged back against him.

"You can't run from me." He moved his hands to her breasts and tweaked her nipples. Heat flooded her core, and he slipped a finger under her stretchy pants to her slit, wet with her arousal. "Or this," he whispered. "Not in these anyway."

She wiggled a foot in the muddy flip-flop, trying to break the intense connection she felt with him, had always felt with him. "No, Luke. You can't do this."

His answer was to rub his thumb over her clit.

She squirmed. "Luke."

He bit her neck. She rose up on tip toes, grinding

into his thumb until she came, screaming his name. When her breath returned to normal, he scooped up her overnight bag, swung her up into his arms like she weighed nothing, and stalked back to the cabin.

After they finished eating the cold bacon and eggs, she set her fork down and frowned. It was time to be logical and clearheaded, which was easier when he wasn't near her. "You don't know me, Luke, if you ever did. And I don't know you."

"That's what this week is for, babe." He shoveled the last bit of eggs into his mouth. "And we actually do," he continued. "Basic human nature doesn't change."

"In the three weeks we were together you got me figured out?"

"Yes," he said, taking the dishes to the sink.

"Lessons learned in the prosecutor's office?" She watched him scrub the egg pan, feeling guilty she wasn't helping. "You win all your cases, do you?"

He handed her the egg pan to dry off. "Proof of what I already knew."

She picked up a dishtowel. "Using that logic, you are somebody who can turn his back on someone without a thought," she said.

He ignored that. "In answer to your second question, yes, I actually have." He rinsed a plate and set it on the drain board. Lexi dried it.

She sighed. "Of course, you do."

"That's what I get paid for, you know, on the tax-payer's dimc."

She hunted through the cupboard to find where the plate went.

Luke's breath hissed as she stretched up toward the top shelf where the plates were stacked.

"Leave it," he snapped. "Sit."

She threw the dish towel on the counter then slumped onto the couch. "Fine."

"Fuck," he said, standing behind her. He rubbed her shoulders. "You're right. We need to talk. But that won't happen if you do that again."

She winced at her sulky voice. "Put a dish away?"

"Yes," he said. "My restraint is gone. All I want to do is sink into you and fuck your brains out."

In her core, her muscles clenched. She got to her knees and turned around to face him. She caressed the bulge between his thighs and undid his fly, pulling his shaft free from his boxers, then licked his balls. He jerked at her touch.

"Lexi," he groaned, his fingers working their way through the sticky strands of her hair, to massage her scalp.

She peered up at him through her eyelashes. "Luke, please, I dreamed of this."

"Holy hell," he said.

She took him as deep as she could. She'd never done this.

"Lexi." He tightened his fingers in her hair. "If you don't stop, I'm going to—"

Her answer was to pull his tight runner's butt closer.

಄಄಄

"Lexi," Luke groaned as his cum shot down her throat and she swallowed all of it.

His hands left her hair and he brought his mouth crashing down on hers. He swung her legs over the back of the couch, so he could lift her into his arms. As he carried her to the bedroom, he resisted the urge to rip her thin T-shirt off. Once in the room, he pulled it over her head. Her shorts didn't fare so well. The material tore as he yanked them down. His clothes followed and he laid her on the bed.

His eyes raked over her sweet body, the body he'd denied himself for so long. She was more exquisite than he imagined. Her nipples were pink and tight like pebbles. Her creamy skin was freckled on her toned shoulders, and her curvy ass tapered to a narrow waist. He caressed her soft, slightly rounded stomach.

She grimaced. "I have to work out more. I hate my stomach."

"It's perfect, you're perfect." He hated the rock hard abs so many women had now. He thought of Lexi's stomach round with his baby. He wanted to make her pregnant and plant his seed in her womb. The thought stunned him. He plunged his tongue into her mouth, the same way he intended to possess her. She was made for him. That probably made him arrogant, but he didn't give a fuck.

Her eyes had gone deep blue.

"You're mine." His hand slipped to her smooth mound and his finger slipped into her pussy, damp with her juices. "This is mine."

⋰⋱⋰

Luke's brown eyes blazed gold and Lexi shivered.

"Are you on birth control, babe?"

She swallowed hard and nodded.

"I know you're clean, the marriage license, unless you had one last fling at your bachelorette party?"

She shook her head.

He nuzzled her neck. "I'm clean, but I understand if you want me to use a condom." His thick cock pressed her juncture.

She moaned.

"Say something."

"I want you, Luke." She almost told him she loved

him. But she couldn't trust him with her heart, not yet. Maybe she should tell him she was a virgin. When his mouth moved to her nipple, she went stupid and no words would come.

"Thank fuck," he rasped. "I can't go slow. I want you too much. Forever I've wanted you."

He entered her in one hard thrust.

She cried out.

He froze. "Lex? You're a virgin? Why didn't you tell me?" He started to draw away from her.

She wrapped her legs around his waist. "No."

His hand cupped her cheek. "I hurt you."

She pressed a kiss to his palm. "It would have hurt, no matter what. Please, Luke." She lifted her hips.

He groaned and filled her again. "Mine," he said. "Only mine." He slid out of her slowly, then filled her, inch by inch, stretching her.

She thrust her hips, desire replacing the ache and rising higher. "Harder, faster."

"Not for your first time." He sucked her nipple until it ached. He soothed it with his tongue before he moved up and captured her lower lip, tugging on it until she parted her lips. His tongue plunged in and out. She met him thrust for thrust. He lifted his head and watched her, as he rubbed his thumb over her swollen, throbbing clit.

She bucked under the avalanche of sensations. How

could he bring her such pleasure? How could she go on with her life when he'd had his fill of her? Why was he the only one she wanted? It wasn't fair.

"What's not fair?"

She bit her lip. She had to stop thinking out loud.

He moved his thumb to pull her lip free. "I love when you think out loud." He continued to finger her clit. "Tell me."

She groaned and shut her eyes. "You're so experienced and I'm—"

He laid his finger over her lips and she opened her eyes reluctantly. "There was a song my parents used to listen to. The refrain goes 'Just how much.' It's depressing as hell. The couple breaks up and the guy marries someone else, but he says he still sees her face when he makes love to his wife." His gaze never wavered. "Babe, I always saw your face."

He pulled out of her, kissed his way down her belly to the juncture of her thighs, and blew on her swollen sex before he plunged his tongue inside her and sucked until she burst into a million pieces.

When she could speak, she ran her fingers over his hard runner's abs. Her voice came in breathy pants. "My parents listened to a song, Tom Petty, I think, 'Free Falling.' That's how I feel now."

Chapter 7

Luke rolled on top of her, his erection sliding through the dampness of her release and nudged her slit. "It ends with you in my arms," he said. "I'm not letting you go."

Hurt clouded her eyes to a shade of bluish gray.

"Talk, babe," he said.

She shut her eyes. "Then why?"

"Look at me Lexi, always look at me," he said.

"I had to see you with all those girls in school, kissing them, when you would never kiss me." Her voice cracked. "And then I had to hear about what you did with them, to them, that you wouldn't do with me."

Christ, his eighteen-year-old self had really fucked things up.

Could he explain and make her understand? Could she forgive him? Could she love him?

"What I felt for you, the way I wanted you, and the way you wanted me, I wanted to fuck you five ways to Sunday. The scary thing was you would have let me."

She set her lips in a thin line and he kissed her hard, tweaking her nipple to a tight pebble. When he lifted his mouth, her eyes had gone dark blue.

Would he ever get tired of staring into her beautiful face? "I was an asshole and a slut. I'm not proud of that. I tried to drive you away. I didn't know how to deal with the gift of what we had and I didn't want to get you pregnant."

He didn't add that he sure as hell did now.

"I was leaving for college. I didn't want you to be the girl who got fucked by Kettering. The thought that some other guy would think he could put his hands on you because I did made me insane. I would have hurt him, babe. And I wanted to give you a choice. I was a whore so you would think you didn't matter to me. I'm not proud of that. It made me physically ill that I hurt you. I saw you flinch when you watched me with those other girls. They meant nothing. It wasn't fair to them either."

She wet her lips. "Marcus," she said.

He grimaced. "Lexi, I'm just going to say this. You're so innocent."

He touched his forehead to hers. "Thank fuck for that. But I made him call off your wedding."

☙❧

"*What?*" Lexi tried to scramble away, but he pressed his weight into her and imprisoned her wrists above her head.

"I know a guy from the office and called in a favor," Luke said.

She squirmed underneath him and he groaned. The feel of his erection at the juncture of her thighs, made her boneless and pliant. What was the matter with her? It was as if he had enslaved her body.

"If you keep doing that—" he groaned. "I want to tell you this. You need to know that Max—"

"Marcus," she said.

He kissed her hard. "I can't stand hearing his name on your lips. What's-his-ass goes both ways, babe. He had no plans to end it with his guy, even after you got married. You were going to stay at Sandals in the Bahamas for your honeymoon, right?"

She nodded.

"His guy lover was going too. He flew out yesterday."

What was she, a loser magnet? How could she be so stupid not to see that?

"Nothing's wrong with you," Luke said. He kissed her fast and hard.

She *had* to stop thinking out loud.

"You're fucking perfect. If you don't think out loud, I won't know what's going on in that amazing brain of yours."

Her brains were scrambled and she couldn't catch her breath. "Let me up, Luke."

"Lexi."

"Please," she said.

He eased his weight off her and she scrambled off the bed.

"I need to think. I want to talk to Reeni."

"I'm not sure about the cell signal," he said.

She slipped on the shorts and then the T-shirt. It was long enough to cover the small tear Luke made in the seam of her shorts when he'd ripped them off her. "I need shoes, the pair you locked in your glove box. And how did you find out about Marcus's significant other? Or where we were going on our honeymoon?"

Luke ran his fingers through his hair. "A cop I know helped me out." He put his hands on her shoulders.

She shook him off.

"He just followed him. He had lunch with Marcus's guy and they talked. Then the cop found his plane and hotel reservations."

"I need some air," she said.

"Okay." He brought back her ballet bridal shoes. "You stay here," he said. "I'll go for a run. The mosquitoes are bad. There's no cell reception."

"You'll get chewed up," she said. She was pissed at him, dammit, so why did she care?

"They don't bother me." He shrugged. He put his keys in the pocket of his cargo shorts, which hung low on his hips, and caught her staring. "Or I could stay." He smiled. "We could watch a movie."

Her anger evaporated. She knew in her heart and gut that Luke was telling the truth about Marcus. She had just been too stupid to see the signs.

Marcus had often mentioned how anti-gay his parents were, so he must have decided to make her his cover.

She was pissed with herself and her female pride was wrecked. Luke seemed to want her now, but he'd turned his back so easily on her before. How could she hope to hold his or any man's interest?

"I'll go," Luke said.

"No," she said. "A movie would be good. Is there anything to drink? The stronger the better."

He went into the kitchen, came back with two cans of Canadian lager, and set them on the coffee table. "This is all there is." He flipped through a stack of DVDs, found one, and looked at her with a frown.

"What?" She popped open their beer can and set them on coasters.

"*Gran Torino*," he said.

She gave a bitter laugh. It was the movie they saw on their first date. Because it had been shot in Detroit, they thought it would be cool to see Clint Eastwood in the grittier parts of their hometown.

She shrugged, taking a long sip of beer. "Why not?"

He started the movie and sat on the couch. He put his arm around her shoulders and pulled her close, just like he did on their first date. As the movie started, he kissed her hair.

Why was she remembering every stinking detail of their past? Would he pull her onto his lap halfway through the movie like before?

They never made it to the ending. And later, she refused to ever watch it again.

She went to take a sip of her beer, but it was empty.

"Take mine." He moved his other hand to her bare thigh.

"Thanks." She took a long swallow. If she had beer breath, maybe he wouldn't want to kiss her.

He took the can out of her hand and drank the rest. "I always want to kiss you," he said.

Shit. Was she thinking out loud again? "It will be nice to actually see the ending," she said, trying to sound snarky. "I hear the car makes it, but Clint doesn't."

Luke's hand caressed her thigh and she tried not to react, breathing deep in and out yoga-style.

"Don't count on it, babe." He nipped her ear, then he pulled her onto his lap at the exact point of the movie as he had done years before.

Even knowing better, she went willingly. "Why, Luke?"

"I remember, too," he said. He kissed her and she went boneless, exactly like she had at sixteen, when she was stupid in love with him…

&〜〜

She'd seen him one day in the library behind the stacks, some senior girl pressed close to him. Luke had looked past the girl, caught Lexi staring, and shrugged the other girl off.

Lexi hadn't waited around, but had walked away as fast as she could. He followed her to her locker.

She had looked past him. "Where's your girl-friend?"

He had twirled a lock of her hair, curling the wave she hated so much around his finger. He pinched the strands. "It's so soft and shiny, natural blonde, too, I think."

She had gone stupid, quiet, and just stood there, unable to move or pull away from him. Finally, she had managed, "Yes."

He had let go of her hair and trailed his thumb across her cheek, to her lips. "And your lips are natural. I like that." He had taken hold of her chin and brushed his lips across hers. "I don't have a girlfriend," he said. "Give me your phone."

Mesmerized, she had pulled it out of her pocket and held it in her nerveless hand.

He had added his number to her contacts, hit call, and handed it back to her. "What's your next class?"

"Spanish."

"*Te gusta*," he said and left her.

Giddy at the idea he liked her, she had hurried across the building to Spanish class. When she had taken her seat after the bell rang, she had murmured, "*Lo siento*."

When school had ended, she stood in line for her bus. Someone had taken a firm hold of her arm.

It was Luke. "Want a ride?"

He hadn't waited for her response, but had steered her toward the parking lot. He opened the door of his jeep and helped her scramble in. After he'd gotten in, he leaned over and pressed his lips to her mouth. He had run his tongue across the seam of her lips then slipped it inside.

Pulling back, he touched her cheek. "Your first one?" he asked with a smile.

"No." She had been kissed twice before, but they had been nothing like Luke's.

"Almost?" His fingers had caressed the nape of her neck. "Suck like this." He had kissed her again, and she had met his tongue boldly until he had broken off the kiss. "I wondered how you'd taste." His voice had sent shivers over her. "Where to, babe?"

She stared at him, still stupid from his kiss, before taking a deep breath to clear her head and blurting out her address.

He drove her home, but didn't kiss her again.

"Thanks," she had said.

Her parents had still been at work, and she wasn't supposed to have boys over if they weren't home. So she had gathered her stuff and gone inside.

She had ignored her algebra homework and filled page after page of her journal with Luke, his brown eyes with flecks of gold, the way he smelled, the way he tasted, how he took hold of her, and how she went boneless and stupid when he touched her.

He texted her after dinner that night. *Want to see "Gran Torino"?*

In the empty months and years to come, the words in her journal would taunt her.

She'd walked out of that movie as if in a dream,

November's bitter chill unable to touch her. For the next two weeks he walked her to all her classes, but he wouldn't kiss her.

He saved those for when they fogged up the windows of his car in the school parking lot.

Then the Friday after Thanksgiving, he came to her house while her parents had been out shopping for Black Friday deals.

She'd pulled him downstairs away from her giggling sisters. She and Luke shot a game of pool on her dad's pool table. She sucked at it, and Luke sank every shot. After one game she'd switched on the TV and flopped down on the old leather sectional.

"Come on," Luke said. "One more."

"No," she pouted. "I hate pool."

Luke seemed reluctant to sit down.

"What's wrong?" she said. "There's no cable down here, but I won't pick a chick flick, I promise. You can watch football if you want."

She hated football, but she would have watched grass grow if it would keep him close to her.

"Okay, babe." He adjusted his pants and sat down, not quite touching her. She noticed the bulge in his pants then.

"Oh," she said. "Here." She handed him the remote. "You have the power." She giggled nervously then cringed. She sounded like a little girl.

He took the controller and kept his eyes on the screen. "I wish," he muttered.

She touched his arm. "You wish what?"

"I wish you, we, were older." He stood up and picked up a pool stick. "You're so innocent and sweet. I should run a mile right now. You make me so hard I can't think."

"Sorry," she said.

He put down the cue stick, sat down, and pulled her onto his lap so her back faced him. She tried to turn sideways but he wrapped his arms around her waist to hold her still. "For the love of God, don't squirm, Lexi, unless you want your first time to be on your parent's basement couch with your sisters listening."

She had stiffened in his arms. Did he think she had no backbone? That he could do whatever he wanted to her?

"Yes," he had murmured against her ear.

She gasped. She said that out loud?

"You would let me leave marks on your body your parents could see. You would let me put my hands and mouth wherever I want on your delectable body. And you would let me take your sweet innocence on this floor if I wanted. You're begging me to right now." He sounded pissed. "Is it like this with other guys?"

Stunned, she could only shake her head.

He sighed and slipped his hands under her sweater

and bra, then palmed her breasts. He had tweaked her nipples and she bit back a moan. "Has anyone else done this?" he'd growled.

"No."

"These are mine." His hand left her breasts and slipped inside her jeans, to burrow under her granny panties to the soft curls covering her sex. "Or this?"

She had shook her head.

"This is mine." He had trailed kisses along her neck then slipped a finger inside her folds. She was wet and slick even as confusion ran rampant. She was acting like a slut.

"Nothing's wrong with you, babe."

She had realized she'd spoken out loud again and clamped her lips shut.

"You don't want this with anyone but me, right?"

"No, I mean, yes, only you Luke."

"Then you have nothing to be ashamed of. I knew you were mine the first time you looked at me."

"Really?" She'd tried for snarky, but missed.

"Really," he'd whispered.

Chapter 7

Lexi woke, unable to remember the end of the movie or how she got to bed. Luke's arm was wrapped around her waist. Why did this feel so right? He stirred and she felt his erection. They were both naked and a thin summer breeze whispered over her skin.

He sighed and pulled her closer. "Lexi."

"How did I get here?" she asked.

"Hmmm." His hand cupped her smooth mound. "I like," he growled and turned her onto her back so he could kiss his way down her belly and tease her slit. He lifted his head and his eyes blazed gold. "Whose is this?"

She moaned.

He slid two fingers inside her and pressed his thumb on her sex. "Whose pussy is this?"

She still couldn't say the words he wanted to hear.

He lapped her sex with his tongue, regaining her attention. "You don't come till I say," he said. He brought her to the verge and then stopped.

She rubbed against him, mindless. "Please, Luke."

She moved her hand toward her clit. He grabbed her wrists and held them above her head.

"I'll tie you to this bed," he said.

Wetness gushed out of her at his words. What was *wrong* with her?

He thrust into her. "You like the thought of being restrained, of me restraining you." He pulled out and thrust hard. "I would never hurt you, babe."

"You did," she said.

He pulled out slow and she whimpered. She was pathetic.

"What do you want?" he said.

She was panting and sticky with sweat. The better question was what did he want? He'd stripped her bare in every way until there was only her love for him.

Luke held his breath.

She saw her need mirrored in his eyes. That was when she knew he needed her to say the words as much as he needed his next breath. He was as much hers as she was his.

He waited.

She smiled and wrapped her legs around his waist. He shuddered and she giggled, heady with her power. "Yours, Luke, I'm yours, you arrogant ass."

He kissed her and she tasted herself. "Whose pussy is this?"

"Yours."

He parted her folds and surged inside. She squeezed her inner muscles, holding him tight. He groaned and plunged farther into her, hitting the wall of her womb. She squealed. "Did I hurt you?"

She shook her head.

"I want to make you pregnant, repeatedly," he said, his mouth poised above hers. "Ever since you looked at me that first time. I would have ruined your life. I wasn't strong enough to control this with you." He plunged inside her, hitting her sweet spot.

She shimmered with her climax.

"Not like I could with other women," he said when her head cleared. He was still hard inside her. "They meant nothing to me. None of them could touch you."

She moaned, and then bit her lip. "I want that, too."

His eyes blazed gold and his body went rigid. "Other men, is that what you mean? To get even?" He cupped her face. "Forget it. Anyone but me touches you and they're gone. Your experience ends with me."

She caressed his back and he seemed to calm a bit.

"I meant I want your babies. I only want you."

He dropped his forehead to hers and they shared the same breath.

"But I want to write, Luke."

He put his finger over her lips. "You're a brilliant writer."

Her eyes grew wide. "How do you know?"

He chuckled. "I stalked you on the Internet. I've read everything you wrote that I could find online."

She nipped his finger and then sucked it hard. "I love you, Luke, but I will make you pay for making me wait so long." She sucked his neck hard, marking him.

"God, babe, I hope so."

⁊∽⧉∽⧉

"Luke, we have to find Marcus's ring. I need to give it back. It's only right," Lexi said.

They ate eggs and bacon, driven out of bed by their howling stomachs. Luke finished his last bit of eggs. "Fuck the ring and fuck Marcus. Scratch that. You are only mine to fuck. Text him and ask how much it cost. I'll write him a check."

"No, Luke. We have to find it. Someone crafted it and mined the diamond. It's beautiful."

Fury roared through him.

"We could at least donate it."

His anger faded as he studied the woman who belonged to him. Her hair hung in soft golden waves framing her heart-shaped face, free of makeup. "We'll go look for it later."

He left and got the small box he'd purchased a year ago out of his glove box. She was rinsing dishes at the sink. He shut off the faucet and pulled her into the living room.

She looked puzzled. "Aren't we going outside?"

"Later." He pulled the ring out of his pocket and took a deep breath. He could do this. He faced juries and judges every day. So why was he nervous about this? "Alexis."

Lexi laughed.

He sank down on one knee.

She gasped.

"You're mine. I'm not letting you go. I applied for a marriage license online. I can pick it up next week if you want to get married here with your family. Or we can go to Vegas tomorrow. We can wait a bit, but not too long. You've missed some pills, I think."

She gasped again.

He opened the box.

She stared at the ring.

"If you don't like this one, we can change it."

She scowled. "Say the words, Luke." Her eyes turned midnight blue. "And not like a plea deal."

"Marry me, Lexi."

꼉꼉

Luke's eyes blazed. This man she loved so much was incapable of asking her to be his wife, so he said the words as a directive. She loved his dominance, but she couldn't submerge herself completely or there would be nothing left but a shell.

"I won't always do what you want," she said. "We have to talk about things before you just take over."

"Is that a yes?"

She giggled. "Do I have a choice?"

His eyes raked over her possessively. "No," he said flatly. "But I don't either. I can't live without you. You're moving in with me until we make it legal."

She frowned.

He swallowed hard, "Okay?" he asked.

"Yes, I'll marry you, and yes, I'll live with you. I can't live without you either. I've been only half alive. I realize that now. It's why I missed the signs with Marcus. I just didn't care. I was going through the motions hoping it would make me happy."

He stood and slipped the solitaire ring on her finger, then pressed her into his erection. "I love you, Lexi." He sucked on her bottom lip, then traced her lips with his tongue. She wrapped her legs around his waist, and he walked to the bedroom. "How many kids do you want?" he said as he spread her out on the bed.

"Let's start with three," she said.

He kissed her hard and she shivered at his passion. How had she lived without him? She tore her mouth away to take a breath and rubbed her sex against him.

He growled and impaled her.

"I'm still making you pay," she gasped.

"I'm the only man who touches you, ever." He sucked the sensitive spot on her neck near her shoulder.

"In other ways," she murmured, clenching her muscles around his hard shaft. "Like this."

His eyes glittered.

She ran her hand over his defined chest and tweaked his nipples. "And this, repeatedly." She nipped his earlobe hard.

He pressed his thumb to her throbbing sex. "You can have your wicked way with me to a point, babe."

"Control freak," she gasped.

"You love it," he said.

She sighed. "I know."

About the Author

Tara Eldana, pen name, is an award-winning staff writer for a weekly community newspaper chain in metro Detroit. She became hooked on romance fiction when her eleventh grade English teacher rejected the book report she wrote, saying the book was much too easy for her, and insisted she read and report on Daphne du Maurier's *Rebecca*. She had read Margaret Mitchell's *Gone With the Wind* that previous summer.

Eldana took a long road through J-school, graduating from Oakland University in Rochester, Michigan in '95, just shy of 20 years after she finished high school, raising a couple kids, working part-time, and doing her homework while her husband and kids watched TV. Still she found time to read what her kids called her "mush books."

She loves the romance genre and loves letting her characters take control of their stories. Eldana is a member of the Greater Detroit Romance Writers of America.